RSPCA

Animal Tales

Dog in Danger!

Other books in the
RSPCA ANIMAL TALES series

Dog in Danger!

Jess Black

RANDOM HOUSE AUSTRALIA

A Random House book
Published by Random House Australia Pty Ltd
Level 3, 100 Pacific Highway, North Sydney NSW 2060
www.randomhouse.com.au

First published by Random House Australia in 2012

Addresses for companies within the Random House Group can be
found at www.randomhouse.com.au/offices.

National Library of Australia
Cataloguing-in-Publication Entry

Author: Black, Jess
Title: Dog in danger!/Jess Black
ISBN: 978 1 74275 336 2 (pbk)
Series: Black, Jess. Animal tales; 5
Target Audience: For primary school age
Subjects: Dog rescue – Juvenile fiction
Dewey Number: A823.4

Cover photograph © Eric Iseelée/Shutterstock
Cover and internal design by Ingrid Kwong
Internal illustrations by Charlotte Whitby
Internal photographs: image of cat by iStockphoto; image of horse
by Lenkadan/Shutterstock; image of dog by Patricia Doyle/Getty
Images; image of terriers by Jerry Young/Getty Images
Typeset by Midland Typesetters, Australia
Printed in Australia by Griffin Press, an accredited ISO AS/NZS
14001:2004 Environmental Management System printer

Random House Australia uses papers that are natural, renewable
and recyclable products and made from wood grown in sustainable
forests. The logging and manufacturing processes are expected to
conform to the environmental regulations of the country of origin.

Chapter One

It was a wonderful summer morning and the day was filled with endless promise. The sky was blue with not a cloud in sight. The surrounding bush smelled just like the Aussie bush should – a special blend of eucalyptus and earthiness. The cicadas and birds competed in their attempts to drown each other out.

Cassie Bannerman sighed contentedly. What a great way to start her weekend. She loved getting out into the bush, especially at sunrise. The same couldn't be said for her friend Ben Stoppard!

'Remind me again why we had to get up so early?' Ben groaned. He rubbed the sleep from his eyes as he stumbled along the dirt track behind Cassie.

'Best time of the day for bird-watching,' said Cassie as she glanced back at Ben and chuckled. He looked as if he'd just dragged himself out of bed and thrown on any crumpled clothes he could find.

This is exactly what *had* happened when Cassie had arrived to pick him up for their bushwalk!

'It wasn't that early,' said Cassie as she

continued walking. 'It was eight o'clock by the time I got to your house.'

'Eight o'clock on a Saturday is like six o'clock on a school day. Nobody gets up that early!' announced Ben as he gave a yawn.

'Come on, Ben,' teased Cassie. 'If you move any slower, you'll go back in time.'

'I wish I could,' muttered Ben. 'Then I'd still be asleep in bed!'

'Don't let Ben's case of wrong-side-of-the-beditis get you down, Cassie!' called Dr Joe, Ben's dad, who was bringing up the rear. 'I love being out in nature!'

Unlike his son, Dr Joe Stoppard enjoyed getting up early in the morning and had a large spring in his step. He was Abbotts Hill's vet and worked at the local RSPCA clinic.

Spurred on by Dr Joe's enthusiasm, Cassie picked up her pace. She was excited about the school project they were embarking on for their social studies class. Mr Harris was one of her favourite teachers and she really wanted to impress him.

The assignment called for them to use a compass and map and go for a bushwalk, recording whatever they saw and heard along the way. Cassie loved bushwalking. She hoped to spot some of the wedge-tailed eagles she knew nested up by the ridge.

Cassie and Ben were lucky enough to live close to some local bushland, and Dr Joe was happy to accompany the kids. Although dogs were allowed on leashes in this state park, they had decided it was best to leave their furry friends at home. They had left Dr Joe's car in the parking area and were about thirty minutes into their walk.

'I'm pretty sure we turn right,' said Cassie as she paused to check the map. They had reached a fork in the path and she wasn't entirely sure which direction to take. Cassie looked over at Ben. 'Wakey, wakey! The compass?'

Ben sleepily pulled a small object from inside his pocket and held it out to Cassie. 'This thing?'

'Yes, that thing!' exclaimed Cassie. 'Were you listening at all in class?'

Ben shook the compass in his right hand and squinted at it. 'I don't think my brain has woken up yet.' He shrugged and held it above his head. 'Can we even get a signal out here?'

'It's not a mobile phone,' Cassie retorted. 'It doesn't need a signal to work. It works using the earth's magnetic fields.'

Ben sighed. 'Speaking of phones, I could use my GPS for directions and we could follow those.'

'That would be cheating,' pointed out Dr Joe, his brows furrowed. 'And don't ask me for help, I'm not really here.'

Ben sighed again and tapped at the face of the compass. 'Or I could add a compass app to my phone. Then at least I'd still have contact with the outside world.' He held the compass out to Cassie in exasperation. 'This thing is, like, one hundred years old.'

'It's a lot older than that,' said Cassie. She gave Ben a pointed look. 'Ancient technology didn't stop explorers using it to discover the world.'

Ben stifled a yawn. Fine, he got the message. When a girl compared you to Captain Cook in front of your dad, then it was time to wake up! He checked the dial again and waited for the needle to stop spinning, but once it had, he found himself no less confused.

'I think we should take the right-hand path,' he announced to Cassie, doing his best to sound confident.

'Excellent choice!' Dr Joe clapped his hands together with enthusiasm.

The trio continued walking, and as they followed the path Ben began to relax and enjoy himself. The bush really was beautiful. They were surrounded by scrubby trees and scraggly bushes dwarfed by huge gum trees, and delicate little bush flowers in myriad colours. It was a stunning time of year to be out in the great outdoors.

'Florence loves the bush,' said Ben. 'It feels weird to be out walking with no big fluffy dog on a lead.'

'I feel the same way,' said Cassie. 'It's like I'm missing an arm or something.'

'Although, knowing Florence, we'd lose her and have to spend the whole day searching,' smirked Ben.

The friends shared a smile. Dr Joe grunted in agreement. Ben's sheepdog Florence was a bundle of mischief and was constantly getting her owners into hot water.

'And the dogs would scare off any

chance we have of seeing wildlife,' said Cassie, thinking about her beloved bitser, Ripper.

'I remember one time at our old place, Florence worked out how to open the gate,' Dr Joe said, smiling at the memory. 'Early one morning we got a phone call from a farmer in Meadow Vale asking if we owned a dog called Florence. Turns out she was making herself completely at home on his couch and we hadn't even got up yet, let alone noticed she was missing. When we picked her up, she didn't even have the decency to look sheepish! We had to make sure that we always had a lock on the gate after that escapade!'

Dr Joe's story reminded Cassie about Ripper as a puppy. 'Ripper was the cutest pup you've ever seen and he knew it. He had the whole neighbourhood wrapped around his little paw. Neighbours used to drop by to give him treats. We had to put a stop to it after we realised he needed to go on a diet!'

'Poor Ripper.' Ben chuckled.

Cassie shook her head, laughing. 'He'd never forgive me if he knew we were out in the bush without him.'

'I won't say a word,' promised Dr Joe with a finger to his lips.

Cassie paused and cocked her head. She was sure she could hear voices calling out a name. She turned to the others. 'Can you hear that?'

'What?' asked Ben.

'Sshh!' whispered Cassie. 'Listen.'

Ben stood quietly. Cassie was right; in the distance they could hear the sound of voices.

'Do you think someone's lost?' asked Cassie.

Dr Joe shrugged. 'Only one way to find out.'

The three bushwalkers continued walking in the direction of the voices.

Chapter Two

A tall man with dark brown hair streaked with grey came into view. He was wearing long shorts and a buttoned-up short-sleeved top and sturdy hiking boots. He looked as if he did a fair bit of bushwalking. He didn't notice Cassie, Ben and Dr Joe at first, as he was too busy speaking to his companions.

'Come on, team, let's get moving,' he barked.

Two other figures came into view: a woman with shoulder-length blonde hair wearing the same kind of practical hiking clothes as the man, and behind her a young girl who looked about the same age as Ben and Cassie.

The girl had the same colour hair as the woman, but it was cut short into a neat bob. She was tall and lanky like the man and woman, who Cassie assumed were her parents.

'Snowy!' called the girl. Her face was flushed, as if she had been crying.

'Snow-y!' cried the woman.

'Good morning,' Cassie said with a bright smile. The three walkers turned at once and were surprised to see Ben, Cassie and Dr Joe.

Ben gave them a little wave. 'G'day.'

'I'm sorry,' said the man. 'We didn't see you there.'

He was about to make introductions when the young girl almost pushed her mother over as she ran down the path towards the others.

'Hello,' she panted. 'Have you seen a golden labrador anywhere along the path?'

Cassie thought the girl's face was familiar, but she couldn't quite place her.

Ben shook his head.

'No, sorry,' said Cassie. 'Why?'

'We were taking her out for a walk when she caught the scent of something and took off,' the girl explained. 'She was on a lead but she took me by surprise and pulled it right out of my hand.'

'And now we can't find her!' said the woman sadly.

Cassie, Ben and Dr Joe listened to their story with concern. A lost dog out in this bush could be serious, especially on a day that was promising to be a hot one, with no water or food.

Cassie and Ben exchanged a glance. Cassie knew Ben was thinking the same thing. These guys needed their help. All thoughts of their school project vanished. They both turned to Dr Joe.

'Don't worry, Eliza,' the woman said as she put an arm around her. 'We'll find Snowy. Your father and I will do everything we can.'

The name Snowy rang a bell with Cassie and all of a sudden it came to her.

'I remember you!' she exclaimed. 'We were at the same dog-training class. It was a few years ago. I have a dog named Ripper. We were paired up for a session.'

Eliza's face lit up. She nodded. 'That's right! I could never figure out why you were in the class. Your dog was already so obedient!'

Dr Joe held out her hand to Eliza's father. 'I'm Joe, and this is my son, Ben. We live just near you guys, in Abbotts Hill.'

'I'm Tom Kennedy, and this is my wife, Nadine,' said Tom as they shook hands. He looked anxious to continue his walk. 'You already know Eliza.'

'You're a year below me at school, aren't you?' Cassie asked Eliza.

Eliza nodded. 'Yes, but I go to Sacred Heart.'

Tom glanced at his watch. 'It's nice to meet you all, but we should be getting on.'

'You're right, Tom, we should,' exclaimed Nadine.

'Perhaps we can help?' asked Dr Joe.

'Thanks for the offer,' said Tom, 'but we've been searching for hours. I think we need professional assistance.'

'My dad works for the RSPCA,' explained Ben.

Tom broke into a big smile. 'Well, that is unexpected! Aren't we lucky that we ran into you.'

'I'll need to ask you a few questions,'

said Dr Joe as he pulled a battered notebook and pen from his pocket.

'Anything!' exclaimed Nadine. 'As long as you can help us find our dog!' She glanced at her husband and daughter. Things were looking up!

Chapter Three

'Snowy is ten years old,' said Nadine, 'but still fairly lively for her age.'

'I hope someone says that about me when I'm the same age in human years,' said Dr Joe with a smile. He winked at Eliza, and then continued with his questions. 'How long has she been missing?'

Tom checked his watch. 'About two hours.'

'Has she ever done anything like this before?' asked Dr Joe.

The Kennedys shook their heads. 'She's a real homebody,' explained Nadine. 'I don't know what got into her.'

'It's my fault,' said Eliza in a quiet voice.

'No, it isn't, Eliza,' said Dr Joe. 'Remember, even the most domesticated animals have instincts they can't control. She probably caught a whiff of rabbit and took off. Snowy was just being a dog, doing what dogs do.'

Eliza nodded but didn't look overly convinced.

Luckily there was enough reception on Dr Joe's phone for him to call the RSPCA headquarters and lodge a report of the missing dog. While he spoke to the RSPCA, the others sat on a nearby cluster of rocks and waited.

They sat in silence until Ben's tummy gave a loud growl. He blushed and Cassie laughed.

'Ben is pretty much ruled by his stomach,' explained Cassie. 'The only way to get him out here was to bribe him with pizza from my parents' deli.'

Tom grinned. 'I'm with Ben. We need to keep our strength up.' He opened his backpack and began to pull out several packets of fruit and nuts.

Eliza shook her head. 'I can't eat a thing. Not until we find Snowy.'

Cassie gave her a sympathetic smile.

'I know how you feel, and I'd be the same way if Ripper went missing. But your dad's right. It could be a long day. And I've brought some pretty yummy food from the deli.'

When Eliza eyed Cassie's food, she decided eating was a good idea after all. As they were tucking into the food, she began to open up about Snowy.

'She was an RSPCA shelter dog. Mum and Dad brought her home when I was only two years old. Since then, we've hardly ever been apart!'

'It was all we could do not to let them sleep together in the same bed,' Tom explained, chuckling. 'We compromised by letting Snowy sleep on the floor by Eliza's bed.'

'She snores something shocking but I couldn't move her even if I wanted to,' said Eliza. 'Snowy's an old lady now and it's up to us to look after her.'

'She's an important part of the family, that's for sure,' Nadine added.

'Don't worry,' said Cassie, 'I'm sure the RSPCA will know what to do.'

'Speaking of which . . .' Ben began. He noticed his father had finished his call and shifted over so he could join them. 'What's up, Dad?' Ben asked.

'The good news is we have now alerted the local RSPCA shelters in case a dog matching Snowy's description is brought in. That's a start. Next, we need to put up posters and distribute flyers saying Snowy is lost and asking anyone to contact us if they see her,' explained Dr Joe.

He cleared his throat before continuing. 'I think it's a great idea to keep searching the surrounding bush in case Snowy is still nearby.' He looked to Cassie and Ben before turning to the Kennedys. 'I'm sure I speak for all three of us when I say we'd like to help you in your search.'

'Thank you!' cried Eliza, giving Ben and Cassie a grateful look.

'What's the bad news?' asked Tom, noting Dr Joe's concerned expression.

'We have a lot of land to cover and not a lot of time to do it in,' explained Dr Joe. 'I checked the weather report and they're predicting hot weather and a possible storm for later this afternoon.'

The others took in the news. It was such a beautiful day; it was hard to believe the weather would change so suddenly.

But Cassie knew one thing about being out in the bush, and that was you had to be prepared for anything!

'Perhaps it would be best if I head home and find a photo of Snowy. Then I can get started on the posters and flyers.' Nadine turned to her husband. 'Why don't you and Eliza stay with Dr Joe and help search?'

'Good idea,' agreed Dr Joe. 'I'd also suggest enlisting the help of neighbours and friends and doing some door-knocking in the areas surrounding this bush.'

'All right!' Nadine did her best to give everyone a bright smile. She gave Eliza a hug and kissed Tom on the cheek. 'I'll let you know the minute I hear anything. You'll do the same?'

'Of course, love,' said Tom. He turned to Cassie and Ben. 'Are you sure you're up for this?'

The two friends nodded their heads emphatically. Were they ever!

Nadine clasped a hand to her mouth and let out a small cry. 'I can't believe we forgot to mention this.'

'What is it?' asked Dr Joe.

Tears began to well in Nadine's eyes. 'There's something else about Snowy we've forgotten to mention.'

Chapter Four

After Nadine had gone Dr Joe turned to the others. 'The fact that Snowy is mostly deaf definitely complicates things.'

'You can say that again,' chimed in Ben.

Cassie nodded, looking serious.

'We can't rely on her hearing us call her name. Bright lights can help grab the attention of a deaf dog, so as the afternoon progresses we'll use torches,' added Dr Joe. 'Being deaf also means that Snowy may spook more easily, which increases the risk of possible accidents.'

Cassie noticed Eliza's crestfallen expression and said, 'But perhaps her sight and smell will make up for her lack of hearing?'

Dr Joe nodded. 'Let's hope so.'

He pulled out his mobile phone from his backpack and re-dialled the RSPCA. 'I'll report this new information to headquarters. In the meantime, Tom, could you mark on the map exactly where you lost Snowy?'

While Dr Joe made his call, Tom spread out the large topographical map he had

KEY
road
building
landmark
picnic area
camping
airport
reservoir

taken with him for the walk. He laid it on the ground and knelt down beside it.

'This is where we are now,' he said, pointing to an area on the map and then moving his finger some distance to the edge of the paper, 'and this is where we were when Snowy ran off.'

Between and around those two points was a lot of bushland. Ben strained to make sense of the map, realising that this search might actually help develop the skills that their school assignment was focusing on.

'How can you even read that thing?' asked Ben. 'All I see are a bunch of squiggles. It makes my brain hurt.'

Tom looked up and smiled. 'Many years spent bushwalking and camping.' He ran his finger along a line on the map. 'See here?' he indicated. 'The scale to the side tells us how to measure the distance we'll be travelling.'

Cassie took over. 'You see, Ben, on this map one centimetre equals one kilometre. You can also work out how steep or flat the ground will be by looking at the contour lines, or squiggles as you call them. If the contour lines are close together, then you know that the terrain is steep.'

Tom looked at Cassie with an approving nod.

'It looks as though there's a lot of ground to cover.' Ben gulped. 'And those squiggles look steep.'

'We're heading uphill,' agreed Tom. 'Can I have your compass?'

Ben pulled it out of his pocket and

handed it to Tom. 'Sure. I'm much more comfortable with a GPS system!'

Tom pointed to the needle as it spun around the dial of the compass. 'See how the needle faces north no matter which way I turn?' He turned around in a circle and held the compass out for Ben to see.

Ben pulled a face. 'I still don't understand. How can it do that?'

Tom smiled. 'I'll show you how to use it properly. It's the least I can do to thank you for your help.'

Ben looked relieved. 'That'd be awesome. This bushwalk was meant to be for a school assignment. We have to practise our navigational skills. That's what Cassie and I were doing when we ran into you.'

Tom raised an eyebrow. 'This type of thing was one of my favourite memories of primary school! I love being out in the bush.'

'Don't get me wrong. I like the bush,' said Ben, and then added, 'but I also like sleeping in on Saturdays and watching cartoons.'

Cassie sighed. 'We were headed up to where the eagles nest,' she said, changing the subject.

Tom nodded. 'They nest north and west of here.' Tom's finger traced up and across the map. 'We'll be heading right past there.'

Dr Joe finished his call and soon they were off.

Tom led the way, followed by Ben and Dr Joe with Eliza and Cassie bringing up the rear.

As they walked, Cassie's mind wandered. She tried to imagine how she would feel if it was Ripper they were searching for, but her stomach tied itself into a knot at the thought.

'Tell me more about Snowy,' Cassie asked Eliza.

Eliza thought for a while. 'Snowy loves playing tricks. She especially likes hide and seek. She'll hide behind doorways and leap out at me.'

Cassie laughed. 'She sounds like lots of fun.'

Eliza turned sharply to Cassie. 'She's not a running-away kind of dog,' she said urgently. 'She's happy to fall asleep on your feet and she occasionally chews on a slipper, but she's good at staying at home. Once I forgot to latch the gate, but she just stayed put. That's why I'm so worried.' Eliza's voice faltered as she spoke.

'It sounds as if Snowy is very well looked after,' said Cassie gently. 'If she can find a way to get home to you then I'm sure she'll try her hardest.'

'Maybe . . .' said Eliza quietly. 'What if she can't get home without help? What if she's lying out there, hurt?'

Cassie didn't know what else to say to reassure her new friend. She'd been concerned about exactly the same thing. They walked on in silence.

When Cassie looked ahead she noticed Dr Joe staring up at the sky. She had been vaguely aware that the light was dimming, but she hadn't realised just how dark the sky had become. It was definitely becoming more humid. The clouds around them were dark and heavy. There was no doubt about it; the bad weather they had predicted was on its way.

Chapter Five

'Thanks for letting me know. I'll be in touch.' Dr Joe returned his phone to his back pocket and turned to the others. 'Eliza, your mum has done a fantastic job organising a local search-party. They're out putting up posters and door-knocking around your area.'

'That's great news!' cried Cassie.

'So nobody has seen Snowy?' asked Eliza, an anxious look on her face.

'Not yet,' said Dr Joe gently.

Eliza fidgeted. 'We need to keep looking around here, then.'

Dr Joe glanced again at the heavy clouds above. 'I'm worried about the weather. The latest update confirms the storm is headed this way.'

'Can't we at least go as far as the cliffs?' Eliza asked. 'That's where we lost her in the first place.'

Dr Joe turned to Tom. 'Your call. Have you all brought raincoats? Torches? Food and water?'

Cassie and Ben nodded. Eliza turned to her father, 'Please, Dad?'

Tom thought for a minute, then nodded. 'If we make it quick.'

With a renewed sense of urgency they all fell into line and began the climb up the steep hill, taking it in turns to call out to Snowy. Although they knew that Snowy probably wouldn't hear them, they felt better calling out her name.

As they walked, the scrubby bush gradually began to thin out and the rocky ground became more prominent. After about twenty minutes of climbing the bush fell away to reveal open ground, which ended in a rocky precipice and a sharp descent into the valley below.

'It's quite something, isn't it?' breathed Tom as they approached. 'Never ceases to impress me.'

'Do you do lots of bushwalking?' asked Cassie.

'Whenever I get the time. I used to be a big rock-climber and abseiler. Now it's more about the scenery . . . Like you, Cassie, I like wedge-tailed eagles.'

Tom pointed to the tufts of grass that dotted the opposite cliff face.

'They love to nest in a prominent position like this, with a good view of the surrounding countryside. Reckon they've got the pick of real estate out here.'

'They're Australia's largest bird of prey,' said Cassie. 'I hope we see one.'

They all gazed at the view beyond. It was a beautiful valley, which rose up again to more bushland and a rocky crevice on the other side. The view was spectacular, but this was rough terrain. It was a reminder that they were well and truly out in the bush and not just a block from home.

'Keep away from the edge,' cautioned Dr Joe as he took a step closer to get a better look below. The rough dirt fell away to an expanse of rocks. All he could see below was rocky ledge after rocky ledge.

'Snowy!' called Dr Joe. 'SNO-WY!' His voice echoed out over the valley.

'Snowy!' cried Cassie. She was soon joined in by Eliza, Ben and Tom.

They all took turns calling out to the dog until finally Dr Joe stopped. The others soon faltered into silence. Gradually their echoes died out just as the first drops of rain began to fall.

'We can't give up!' Eliza blurted out.

'No, we won't do that. Let's just take a break for the night.' Dr Joe gave Eliza a squeeze on the shoulder. 'I can't have you kids out here in the middle of a storm.'

Eliza remained firm. She turned back to the path they had come from. 'If I were lost, Snowy would keep looking for me, I just know it. She wouldn't stop for anything,' the young girl insisted.

'I'm sorry, sweetheart,' said Tom. 'We have to keep you kids safe. We'll look for Snowy again first thing tomorrow, I promise.'

Eliza looked around her, stubbornly refusing to move. The drops of rain were turning into a light drizzle. She wiped the moisture from her face then sighed and fell into her father's outstretched arms for a hug. 'Until tomorrow then.'

The small search party put on their raincoats and turned for home.

As she followed the others, Cassie gave the valley a final glance over her shoulder. Something flashed in the distance and caught her eye. She turned to get a better look.

It was an eagle! A wedge-tailed eagle with its wings outstretched. Here was the massive wing expanse and distinctive long wedge-shaped tail she'd heard so much about. It seemed to be enjoying the droplets of rain as it cruised over the valley.

'Wow!' Cassie mouthed to herself.

For a moment it was just her and the eagle. Then all of a sudden it took a dive.

Cassie lurched forward to see where it had gone. She searched the cliff face below but could see nothing. She turned to Ben, who she thought was beside her, but then realised she was actually alone. The others had gone.

Cassie let out a sigh. Then she heard it – the unmistakeable sound of a dog whimpering.

'Snowy?' she called out. Cassie peered over the edge, but she still couldn't see anything. 'Are you there, Snowy?'

The eagle reappeared and soared away. The whimpering grew louder. Cassie was sure Snowy was somewhere on the cliff face, even though she couldn't see her.

Cassie turned and ran back along the path to catch up to the others. 'Dr Joe! Eliza!' she called. 'I think I've just found Snowy!'

Chapter Six

'Stay well back, kids,' Tom cautioned. He was holding onto Dr Joe's arm so that the doctor could get a better look over the cliff face.

'Snowy!' Dr Joe cried, 'Here, girl!' He waited but there was no sound except for the rain, which was now coming down steadily.

Dr Joe stepped back away from the edge and shrugged. 'I can't see Snowy anywhere, but it's possible she's caught in a ledge or crawled into a corner, out of sight. I can't tell from up here.'

'What should we do?' asked Eliza.

Tom produced a climbing harness from his backpack. 'I could inch my way down the cliff face for a better look.'

Dr Joe studied Tom, concerned. 'You can't go down there in this weather.'

Tom continued with his preparation. 'We can't leave now. We have to find out one way or another if she's down there.'

He began attaching a climbing rope to a sturdy tree nearby. With the rope firmly secured to a large gum tree, he then attached the rope using a series of pulleys and buckles.

Finally, he strapped himself into the harness. Before anyone even had a chance to argue further he gave them a quick wave.

'I'm only going down two metres, tops,' he said with a reassuring grin as he took the slack in the rope and abseiled over the edge of the cliff.

'That looks awesome. Can I try it too, Dad?' asked Ben.

Dr Joe raised a disapproving eyebrow.

'Not now, of course,' said Ben, back-pedalling quickly.

The children and Dr Joe stood side by side, waiting in the rain for Tom to resurface.

All of a sudden a fork of lightning lit up the sky. After a few moments it was followed by a loud crack of thunder.

Eliza grabbed Cassie's arm. 'Snowy's really scared of storms. She'll panic and go nuts.'

'We don't even know for sure that Snowy's –'

The rest of Ben's reply was drowned out by the sound of a loud and sorrowful howl that echoed across the canyon.

'Snowy!' cried Eliza. On impulse she began to move closer to the edge of the cliff, but Cassie and Ben held her back.

A second later Tom's head popped back into view. 'She's down there, all right,' he exclaimed as he pulled himself back onto level ground. 'Would never have seen her if she hadn't got a fright from the lightning. The rapid movement of her golden fur caught my eye. She's about a third of the way down. Somehow she must have fallen and landed on the smallest rock ledge. That dog is very lucky she didn't drop any further down!'

'Dad, that's fantastic!' cried Eliza.

'Only trouble is,' said Tom, 'I have no idea how we're going to get her back.'

Chapter Seven

The lightning moved away from the area, but flashes could still be seen in the distance. Unfortunately steady rain continued to fall. By now they could all hear Snowy. Her cries echoed out into the valley.

'Poor Snowy!' cried Eliza. 'She must be terrified.'

Dr Joe was busy shouting into his mobile phone over the sound of the rain. 'We need backup. We've located the dog, but she's trapped on a ledge on the cliff face.' He lowered his voice and turned away. 'I need to get closer to see her injuries, but I'd guess she needs medical help immediately.'

Cassie overheard the last part of the call. She turned to Tom. 'We have to do something for Snowy!'

'I repeat,' shouted Dr Joe into his phone, 'this rescue has just turned into an emergency situation!' He shook his head with frustration and ended the call. He turned to the others. 'They're mounting a backup operation, but I don't know how much time that will take.'

'If we wait too long, Snowy could

become so frightened she might fall,' Eliza cried. 'You said so yourself, Dr Joe, she's stuck on a ledge.'

'I just don't see what else we can do. We don't have the necessary equipment to send someone down to bring Snowy back up the cliff.' Dr Joe shook his head. He racked his brain for an answer. A big dog and a person could weigh as heavy as one hundred and fifty kilograms and they just didn't have the manpower.

Dr Joe turned to the others suddenly. 'T.L.A.E.R!' he exclaimed.

'I'm sorry?' asked Tom. 'Is that a special RSPCA code?'

'It stands for Technical Large Animal Emergency Rescue!' cried Dr Joe excitedly. 'There's a course being run today, not far from here. One of our inspectors, Richard Nott, is there. It's a long shot, but there's a chance they could bring their equipment and perform the rescue themselves.'

Eliza stared wide-eyed at Dr Joe.

Tom clapped his hands together. 'Fantastic!'

Dr Joe pulled out his phone once again and quickly dialled Richard's number. They waited anxiously to see if he would pick up.

'Richard?' Dr Joe spluttered in relief as he answered. 'There's no time to go into detail but I need you to put what you're currently learning into practice, right now!'

Nobody spoke much as they anticipated Richard's arrival. Half an hour later and the rain had not let up. *Thank goodness we brought wet-weather gear*, thought Cassie.

Finally, just as the kids were starting to lose hope, they saw two men jogging up towards them. They were carrying heavy packs on their backs.

'Richard!' Dr Joe stepped forward eagerly to greet his colleague.

'We came as fast as we could,' puffed Richard.

Richard was shorter than Dr Joe and had a much more solid build. With his fair hair cropped short against his scalp, his piercing blue eyes twinkled with good nature as he fixed his gaze upon each of them in turn. He reminded Cassie of a mountain goat. She decided she liked him immediately.

'This is Andrew,' Richard introduced the other man. 'He's my course supervisor and offered to come and help.'

'We can't thank you enough,' Tom exclaimed. 'It's a bit crazy to be out in this weather.'

'This is exactly what my training was for,' Richard said with a smile. 'You'll be putting me to the test as I do my best to remove a large animal safely from a life-threatening situation. A little rain isn't going to stop me.'

In consultation with Andrew, Richard set about gathering together their equipment and preparing for the rescue. They had brought with them several slings, ropes, pulleys and harnesses. Once they were ready, Andrew strapped Richard into a harness and he placed the harness they would use for Snowy into a pack on his back.

'We're looking at unstable ground, a scared animal and bad weather – we couldn't have given you a better test at the course if we tried!' said Andrew.

'Only it's not a test, it's for real,' said Eliza, feeling shaky.

Tom put his arm around his daughter and drew her close.

'Don't worry, Eliza,' said Richard. 'We'll get Snowy back in no time.'

Richard began inching his way down the drop, with Andrew and Tom helping him to navigate the rope.

Ben caught Cassie's eye. Never in a million years could he have imagined their day would turn out like this. 'I'm not sure this is what Mr Harris had in mind when he set us the bush-orienteering assignment,' he said to Cassie.

Cassie snorted. 'We had better get an A for this project!'

'You're not the only one hoping for a good mark!' called Richard as he disappeared from view.

The friends shared a laugh. It was a way of relieving the tension they were all feeling.

They waited what seemed like forever for Richard's signal, but there was only the sound of rain and wind. Cassie couldn't stand it any longer; she gingerly stepped closer to the edge and peered over to check if she could see Richard. But all she saw were wet rocks being pummelled by rain. The light was so dim now it was hard to see anything. Cassie realised it was starting to get dark.

Chapter Eight

'Richard!' called Tom. 'RICHARD, are you okay?' Tom leaned over for a better look, the rope still taut in his hands. It was difficult to see anything, even with Ben and Eliza flashing their torches over the ledge.

Tom turned to the others and gestured to the rope. 'I doubt we'll hear him over the noise of the storm. The rope is our main source of communication from now on.'

Just then a branch from the nearby gum tree snapped and crashed on the ground beside them.

'Come on, Richard,' muttered Tom nervously. 'Hurry up!'

Suddenly the rope went slack in Tom's hands.

Andrew explained what that meant. 'Okay,' he said. 'Richard has made it to the ledge and is going to attach the harness to Snowy.'

Eliza and Ben shone their torches on the rope and waited. Then it sprang to life, giving two sharp tugs before once again growing taut.

Tom nodded as he tested out the

weight of the rope. 'Definitely more of a Snowy weight than a Richard weight.'

'Go, Snowy! You can do it!' whispered Eliza, fingers and toes crossed.

Tom and Andrew began to pull very slowly and carefully on the rope as they drew it back up towards them.

Dr Joe was making his own preparations with the medical kit Richard had brought for him. He signalled to the girls. 'Cassie and Eliza, see what dry clothes we have left and if there's any water available. Snowy will need to be kept warm and rehydrated until we can get her medical attention.'

Cassie and Eliza used one of the torches to scramble through the packs to see what they could find. They were able to fill a food bowl with water and found an extra warm

coat Ben had thrown in as an afterthought. Cassie made a mental note to thank him later on.

'Eureka!' cried Tom as a very bedraggled labrador gradually came into view.

'Snowy!' cried Eliza.

One more pull from Tom and they had her over the ledge. Andrew reached forward and picked up the dog, carrying her over to the gum tree. 'You're in good hands now,' he said soothingly to Snowy as he placed her on the ground. Andrew stepped back and allowed Dr Joe to give her an examination.

'Here, old girl,' said Dr Joe, giving her wet fur a stroke. He used the jacket to dry her off as best he could before he ran his hands expertly over her body. Snowy in turn gave him a good sniffing over just to make sure he was someone to be trusted.

One leg stood out at an odd angle, but she wasn't too distressed. She just looked completely exhausted. Dr Joe gave her some medication to help manage her pain.

Eliza wrapped her arms wrapped tightly around Snowy's neck as she buried her face in her fur. Snowy's tail began a slow, steady wag. 'I'm sorry, Snowy,' Eliza sobbed. 'I should never have let you go.'

Cassie watched as Eliza hugged her dog. Soon, Snowy was panting less heavily and began to lap tentatively at the makeshift water bowl.

'Well done, girl,' whispered Cassie.

'Will Snowy be okay?' asked Eliza anxiously.

Dr Joe nodded. 'Her back leg may be

fractured. I won't know for sure until I do an X-ray. She's very lucky.'

'No more rabbit chasing!' said Eliza sternly as she looked into Snowy's trusting face. Snowy let out a loud huff and lay down on her side. Clearly she didn't think much of the doctor's orders.

'What about Richard?' asked Ben as he flashed his torch over the cliff edge. 'We need to get him back up here too.'

'Of course!' Tom jumped up hastily and unbuckled the harness from Snowy. He checked it was firmly attached to the rope and threw it back out over the cliff. 'Here goes,' said Tom.

They all watched as the remainder of the rope snaked its way back over the edge.

Chapter Nine

'I'm not sure Mr Harris will believe me when he reads what happened on our bushwalk,' said Ben to the others.

'Let's just hope your story has a happy ending,' muttered Tom.

Andrew checked the rope again, but it was still slack. 'Come on, Richard,' he said nervously as he pulled the rope back up in swift loops around his wrist and elbow. 'Here we go again,' he grunted as he threw it out into the distance.

This time the rope grew taut.

'He's got it!' Cassie cried excitedly.

Andrew gave the rope a good tug, but it came loose in his hands. 'Must have been a branch or a jagged rock,' he said grimly. He pulled the rope up and looped it neatly. 'Third time lucky!'

The rope sailed into the air and dropped down the cliff. Cassie, Ben and Tom watched on anxiously. There was a pause before Andrew's arms jerked sharply.

'That's him!' Andrew shouted. He took a deep breath as he steeled himself. Tom was in place behind him as backup.

'Take it easy, Richard,' Tom said to himself. The rope moved around, as Richard must have been attaching the harness, and finally it burst to life with two sharp tugs.

Tom positioned one foot against a sturdy rock and leaned back using his body weight to do the work of supporting Richard. Very slowly, as Richard was climbing up step by step, Andrew drew the rope in towards him.

It seemed that right then everyone arrived at once. Richard's face appeared illuminated by the torchlight coming from the rescue party. Nadine was there with two RSPCA officers. The officers took one look at Andrew and Richard and shook their heads.

'Trust Richard to get here first,' one chuckled.

Andrew and Tom drew Richard up to safety.

'That was one hair-raising practical test, I can tell you!' said Richard.

'You did really well,' praised Andrew. 'Calm under pressure and Snowy definitely seemed to place her trust in you.'

Tom approached Richard. 'I can't thank you enough,' he said, shaking Richard's hand.

'All in a day's work,' said Richard as he dried himself off. 'When else would I find the time to get in a little abseiling practice?' He gave Tom a wink.

The rain had finally eased up. Hot drinks from thermos flasks were passed around.

Cassie sighed as she sipped from her warm cup. 'That's the best hot chocolate I've ever tasted.'

The day's events were catching up with her and Cassie couldn't help but let out a yawn.

'Now who's yawning?' teased Ben. 'You morning people are terrible once the sun goes down.'

Cassie rolled her eyes.

'I'm full of beans now. I could do anything!' boasted Ben.

'You can get us home, then,' suggested Dr Joe with a wry smile.

'But it's night-time,' said Ben. 'How will we find our way back?'

Tom clapped him on the back. 'I'll help, but I reckon you can figure it out with

a little help from a map, a compass and a torch.'

Ben groaned. 'Homework! There's just no escaping it!'

Thanks to Ben's newfound navigational skills, they did all make it home and Cassie's parents met them at the park's entrance. Cassie's family opened up the deli specially to serve plates of fresh pasta to everyone involved in the search party.

Snowy snored on a blanket in the corner of the store, with Eliza keeping a close eye on her beloved canine.

'I'll bet Eliza won't leave Snowy's side any time soon,' noted Ben.

Ripper bounded over to Cassie, who gave her dog a huge hug. She didn't even grimace when he licked her face with his big wet tongue. 'Good to see you, boy,' she said as she tickled the back of his ear just the way he liked it. 'Boy, did you miss an adventure and a half!'

RSPCA

ABOUT THE RSPCA

The RSPCA is the country's best known and most respected animal welfare organisation. The first RSPCA in Australia was formed in Victoria in 1871, and the organisation is now represented by RSPCAs in every state and territory.

The RSPCA's mission is to prevent cruelty to animals by actively promoting their care and protection. It is a not-for-profit charity that is firmly based in the Australian community, relying upon the support of individuals, businesses and organisations to survive and continue its vital work.

Every year, RSPCA shelters throughout Australia accept over 150,000 sick, injured or abandoned animals from the community. The RSPCA believes that every animal is entitled to the Five Freedoms:

Fact File

- freedom from hunger and thirst (ready access to fresh water and a healthy, balanced diet)
- freedom from discomfort, including accommodation in an appropriate environment that has shelter and a comfortable resting area
- freedom from pain, injury or disease through prevention or rapid diagnosis and providing veterinary treatment when required

- freedom to express normal behaviour, including sufficient space, proper facilities and company of the animal's own kind and
- freedom from fear and distress through conditions and treatment that avoid suffering.

RSPCA

DEALING WITH LOST PETS

Searching for your lost pet can be a stressful time, but it's important to keep focused and not panic.

If your pet goes missing, you should:
1. Call the RSPCA and report your missing pet.
2. Call the vets in your local area, as a member of the public may have taken your pet to a vet surgery.

3. Call your local council pound to report your missing pet.
4. Do a door-knock of the local neighbourhood from where your pet went missing, as well as letter box drops, putting signs in local shops and broadcasting lost notices on the radio and in newspapers.

You should search for your lost pet as soon as it goes missing as there is a much higher chance of you finding your pet the sooner you start. Even delaying the search a few days can drastically reduce the chance of you finding your pet.

In addition to notifying the RSPCA and council pound, it is also a good idea to go to all the animal shelters and pounds and actually view the lost animals as often as possible.

It's important to continue calling the RSPCA every day so that they can continue to search for your lost pet.

Fact File

To give your pet the best chance of being found:

- Get your pets microchipped — this is important for the registration process and will mean that their ID and your contact details are on record

- Ensure that your pet has their collar and ID tag on them at all times — this will make it a lot easier for you to be contacted should someone find your missing pet

- Always include a secondary contact number on your pet's ID — in the event that you're involved in an emergency, someone else can be contacted in your place.

RSPCA

Animal

Tales

RSPCA Animal Tales

A New Home for Cocoa

Buying this book helps the RSPCA look after animals!

Helen Kelly

RSPCA Animal Tales

Buying this book helps the RSPCA look after animals!

Florence Takes the Lead

COLLECT THEM ALL

COMING DECEMBER 2012